This Book is given with love:

_____

_____

Written by Leigha Huggins

Illustrated by Nino Aptsiauri

Edited by Bobbie Hinman, Karen Austin, and the wonderful Sheri Wall

For all inquiries, please contact us at:
info@puppysmiles.org

To see more of our books, visit us at:
www.PuppyDogsAndIceCream.com

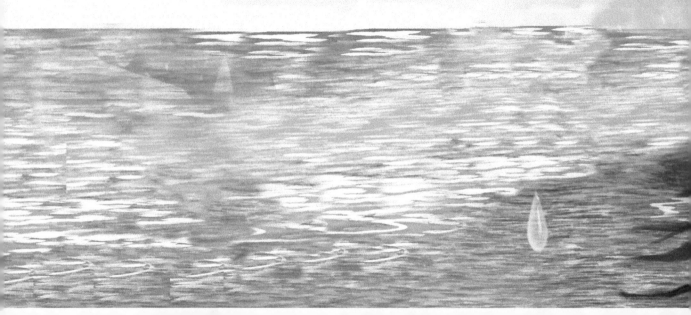

Little Lucy & HER LITTLE WHITE LIES

Written by LEIGHA HUGGINS
Illustrated by NINO APTSIAURI

This story is layered
with lies 'til the end.
To find the real meaning,
you might read it again!

With **tiny white lies,**
the truth no one would know...
At least that's how Lucy
hoped it would go.

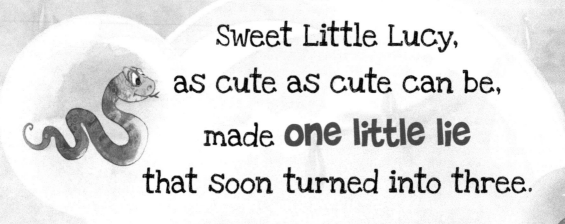

Sweet Little Lucy,
as cute as cute can be,
made **one little lie**
that soon turned into three.

Then one after that...
then another and some more...
becoming a pile
of white lies galore!

with the **layers of lies**
piling high in the sky,
her mother just stared
then had to ask, "Why?"

"Lucy, why are there blankets
piled high on your bed?"
Rather than the truth,
Lucy offered this instead...

"Well, I was chilly
and shivered all night...
So I added **every blanket**
that was in sight."

"You see, out of nowhere,
way up in the sky,
came buckets of water
just dancing on by...

They **splished and they splashed**
as they twirled in the air,
with **a drip and a dribble**
over here and over there."

"I could barely believe
my very own eyes,
as the water continued
to splash and to rise!"

But the lies began spattering
every which way,
as Lucy kept thinking
of more things to say.

Her **little white lies**
just continued right on...
She stopped only once
for a stretch and a yawn.

The Princess
and
the Pee

"That's when, from above, falling out of the sky, came **another Big Blanket** to help keep me dry!"

Though more lies kept swimming
around in her head,
Little Lucy just wanted
to go back to bed.

With all of her effort
and all of her lies,
Big tears Began Pooling
in Lucy's sweet eyes.

Climbing off of her bed,
Lucy's head was hung low,
she was now ready and willing
to give truth a go...

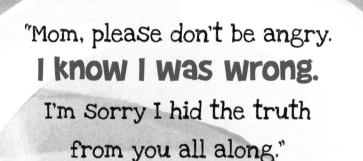

"Mom, please don't be angry.
I know I was wrong.
I'm Sorry I hid the truth
from you all along."

To Lucy's Surprise,
the response she received...
She didn't expect
and she couldn't believe.

"Sweet Little Lucy,
I'm not angry at all,
**But please Don't tell lies,
not Big ones or Small."**

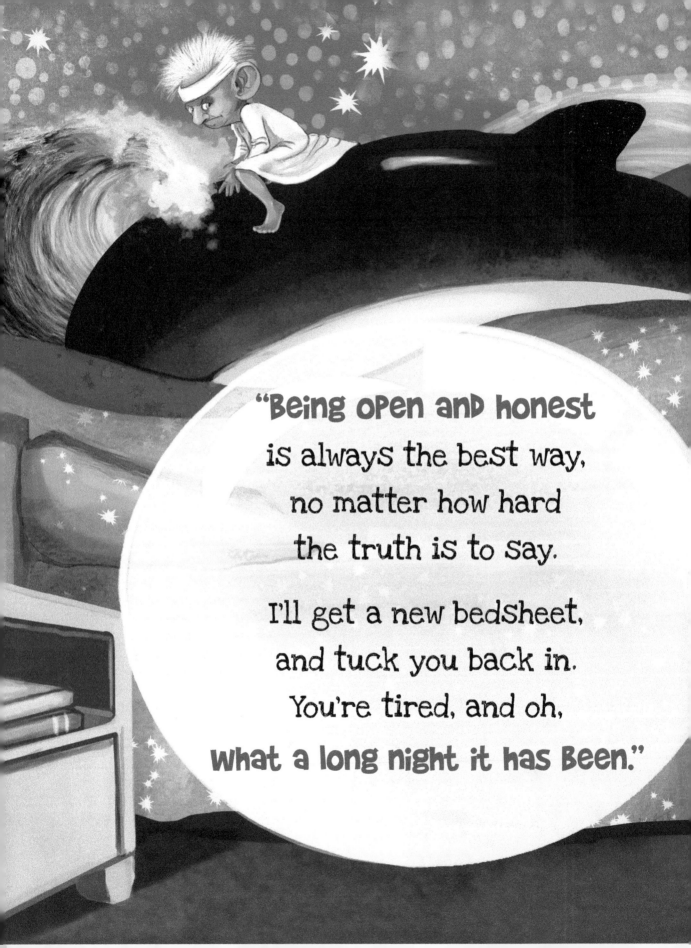

"Being open and honest
is always the best way,
no matter how hard
the truth is to say.

I'll get a new bedsheet,
and tuck you back in.
You're tired, and oh,
what a long night it has Been."

"Sleep well, Little Lucy...
all is now fine.
Sweet Dreams are still waiting,
dear child of mine."

The story's now finished,
you're at the end of the book,
but here's a special message
for mom, take a look!

Thank you, mama, for all that you do,
the cooking, cleaning, and laundry too.
Early mornings accompanied by many late nights,
embracing life's lows and all of its heights.

The comfort, the hugs, the fights with flu bugs,
the owies, the lessons, and all the heart tugs.
They Couldn't, and wouldn't, Do it Without yo
Please know thanks are deserved, without further add

Meet The Author
Leigha Huggins

Leigha Huggins is an enterprising author who is pursuing her
passions for creativity and love, woven with words and illustrations.
Her goal is for her books and the messages they carry,
to be cherished over time. Leigha believes we can do
great things with love, wonderful things with ambition,
and amazing things with intention. We can choose to create beauty
over clutter, memories over mistakes, and love over all.

Meet The Illustrator
Nino Aptsiauri

Nino Aptsiauri graduated from the Faculty of Journalism at Tbilisi State University in Georgia, and continued on to the Faculty of Art History where she received her Certificate in Digital Art.

Nino has been painting and writing since childhood. Her poems and stories have been published in numerous literary magazines and newspapers, and she is now in-demand as an illustrator of children's books. Nino and her family reside in Tbilisi, Georgia.

Enjoy Leigha's story? Check out her other titles!

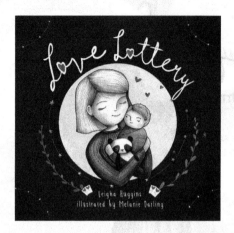 

A relate-able past offers new future outlooks with a creative twist... Analogies are life's stories and lessons waiting to be told from a new perspective... Thank you, Brother, for all your insightful talks, your worldly wisdom and the stories that will never leave me.

- Leigha Huggins

I am so glad that we, as artists, have the opportunity to create children's books that can touch the small, pure hearts of kids and leave an imprint in them forever. We must always strive to be as pure, as sincere, and as sweet as they are.

- Nino Aptsiauri

Claim Your FREE Gift!

Visit ➡ PDICBooks.com/Gift

Thank you for purchasing Little Lucy, and welcome to the Puppy Dogs & Ice Cream family.

We're certain you're going to love the little gift we've prepared for you at the website above.

CPSIA information can be obtained
at www.ICGtesting.com
Printed in the USA
LVHW070843241021
701361LV00002B/24